MW01171324

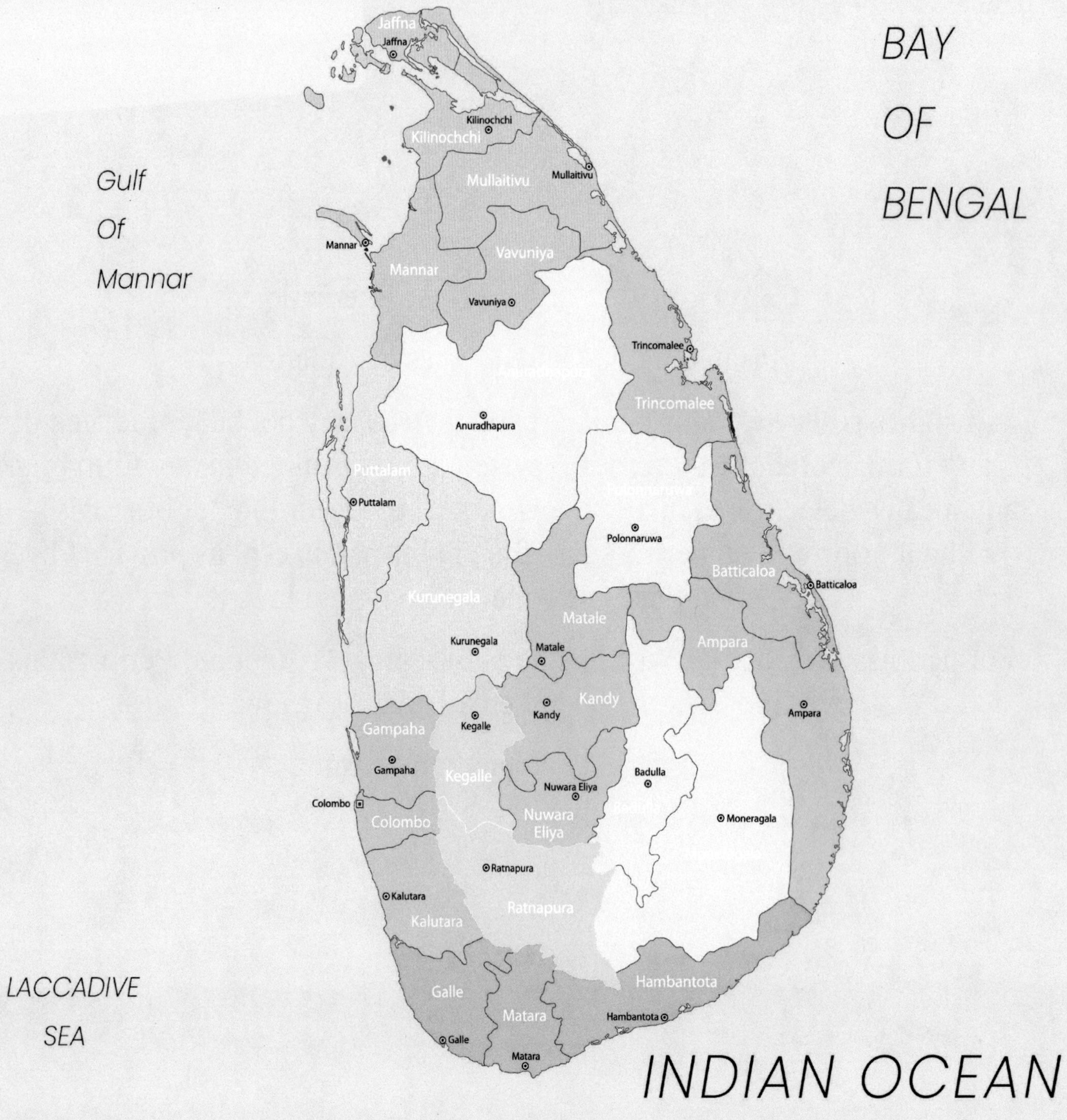

BAY OF BENGAL
Gulf Of Mannar
LACCADIVE SEA
INDIAN OCEAN
Jaffna
Jaffna
Kilinochchi
Kilinochchi
Mullaitivu
Mullaitivu
Mannar
Mannar
Vavuniya
Vavuniya
Trincomalee
Trincomalee
Anuradhapura
Puttalam
Puttalam
Polonnaruwa
Batticaloa
Batticaloa
Kurunegala
Kurunegala
Matale
Matale
Ampara
Ampara
Kandy
Kandy
Kegalle
Kegalle
Gampaha
Gampaha
Colombo
Colombo
Badulla
Nuwara Eliya
Nuwara Eliya
Moneragala
Ratnapura
Ratnapura
Kalutara
Kalutara
Galle
Galle
Matara
Matara
Hambantota
Hambantota

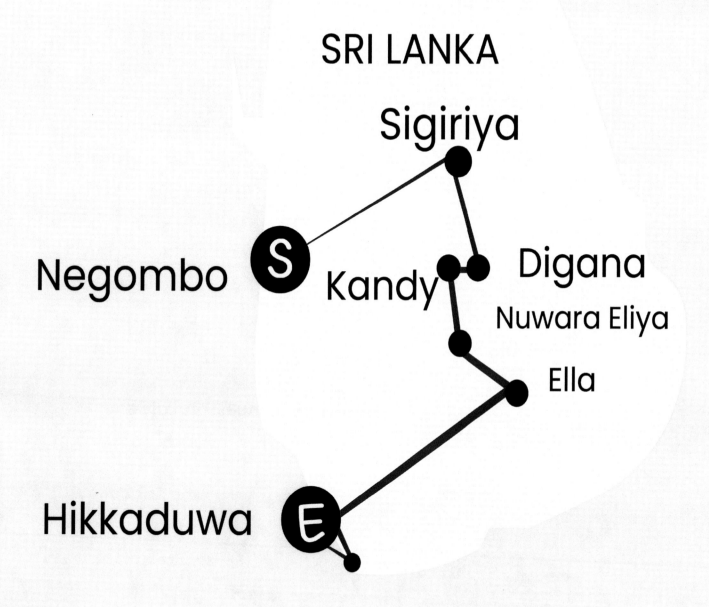

Meet Fernando. He is a private detective. Fernando has a great imagination and a keen mind for piecing together clues.

Ziz is Fernando's parrot. Together, they solve mysteries throughout different countries in the world. They're best friends that always have each other's back in every mystery they solve.

One day, while Fernando is watching the news, he listens as the newscaster shares footage from last year's Kandy Esala Perahera.

What does that mean? Ziz says.

The Kandy Esala Perahera parade is held annually in July and August. In English it means, "The Festival of the Tooth", says Fernando.

The newscaster goes on about the importance of the celebration and cuts to the live coverage of this year's parade in Kandy, Sri Lanka.

The Kandy Esala Perahera, a unique symbol of Sri Lanka, pays homage to the Sacred Tooth Relic of Buddha.

The relic is kept at the Sri Dalada Maligawa or the Temple of the Sacred Tooth Relic in the city of Kandy.

This procession consists of traditional dances like fire dances, the reporter says while gesturing to the food vendors, lights, and street performers around her.

The camera zooms in on a group of fire dancers in the background. Several men sporting orange and white clothing march in a circle while twirling lit torches in their hands.

Then they turn to each other and playfully swing at each other with the fire. Their shoes have bells around them that jingle and chime with their every step.

Fernando and Ziz are enjoying the spectacle before them until a man snatches the microphone from the reporter's hands and turns the camera towards himself.

Woah, what's going on? The reporter asks.

Please, I am looking for Fernando and Ziz. It's urgent! The man says through an interpreter.

Give that back! The newscaster yanks the microphone back and sighs.

No, you don't understand. The Kandy Esala Perahera can't happen this year. The sacred tooth is missing! Please help!

As the man shouts this, the music in the background stops, the fire dancers stop, and the entire crowd pauses to stare at him.

His name is Gayan. He is asking Fernando and Ziz to please come to Kandy, Sri Lanka. He needs their help. Please hurry! Says the interpreter.

Do you hear that Ziz? Fernando asks.

Yes, we're going to the festival! Ziz says with excitement.

Fernando goes to his room and finds Sri Lanka on the world map hanging on his wall.

Ziz, look! Says Fernando. That is where we are going!

Next stop, Bandaranaike International Airport! Let's get our tickets! Fernando shouts with glee. I will take my laptop with me on the plane to read about Sri Lanka, its history, and local languages.

Tell me all about it later! Says Ziz with an excited voice.

The two friends land at Bandaranaike International Airport, also known as Colombo Airport in Sri Lanka.

Once they land, Fernando buys a book that talks about the significance of the Kandy Esala Perahera. He learns enough to help the pair on their journey.

Fernando hires an interpreter, a tall dark man named Pradeep. He has a kind smile and even kinder eyes.

Thank you for joining us on our journey, Pradeep. My name is Fernando and this is Ziz. We are on the case of the missing tooth relic, and we're looking for a man named Gayan.

Of course! I will be happy to guide you to the temple. We are so thankful you are here to help us recover the relic, the interpreter says with a smile.

Pradeep hails a taxi.

They start their road trip to the city of Kandy, over 80 miles away.

On the way over to Kandy Ziz asks, why is this relic so famous?

Fernando turns on his laptop.

Let me show you something very interesting! Says Fernando.
On the airplane, I read about the history of the relic. It goes as far
back as Sri Lankan legends that talk of Buddha's death. In 543 BC,
Buddha passed away, and his body was cremated in a special
sandalwood pyre at Kushinagar, a city famous for Buddhist pilgrimage
sites. Ziz, I know you are going to ask me what pyre is! It is a pile
of wood.

Fernando continues: One of his canine teeth, the left one specifically,
was taken by his follower Khema, a famous female Buddhist nun.
Khema gave the tooth to the king. And ever since, it's been a royal
possession.

Yes, it is sacred to us, and it was believed that whoever possessed
the tooth would rule the land. But the thing is, the relic was crushed
ages ago. Now we celebrate using a replica. If we don't find the relic,
this festival won't happen for the first time in years, Pradeep says
in a panic.

Wow! What an amazing story! How will we find who took it? Ziz
wonders.

They arrive at Kandy.

We must ask around and search for clues. I need to take a closer look at the spot where the man grabbed the reporter's microphone. Where does the parade take place? Asks Fernando.

Just over there, let me walk you to it, Says Pradeep.

Fernando and Ziz follow the interpreter to the location that he was pointing at. It was the same place that they saw on the news.

They notice a crowd of people that are watching the fire dancers and other street performers. Several groups of tourists and locals eagerly await the start of the festival.

Food stalls and street vendors serve all kinds of food, but one dish smells the strongest and attracts Ziz.

Ziz flies over to the stall. Yum, that smells amazing!

Ziz, come on! We can try some food after we solve this mystery; Fernando calls Ziz over to him.

Fernando looks at the stall and sees a delicious setup of roti flatbread, aromatic spices, crispy veggies, and yummy meat.

That's Kottu, a national dish, and popular among locals and tourists. It is made with roti flatbread, spices, crispy vegetables, and great-tasting meat. The bread is made with flour, coconut, green chilies, and onions, Says Pradeep, smiling. I can treat you both to this later if you like.

For sure! Thank you! Says Ziz.

Kottu

Now they see him; the man that was shouting in the crowd, asking for Fernando and Ziz's help.

Fernando runs over to him while Ziz flies overhead. Pradeep joins them and listens to the man speaking in a language that Ziz and Fernando have never heard before.

Fernando, Ziz! Hello. As you know by now, my name is Gayan. I am so thankful that you are here.

How did you know about us? Ziz asks.

Gayan begins speaking in his language.

He says he heard the news about how you two solved the mystery of the gold and jeweled shoe in Malaysia. You must understand how important this relic is to everyone here, and especially to Gayan and the temple members. This is their life's work, Pradeep interprets.

I understand. I am honored to help you retrieve this sacred relic, Fernando says with a smile.

What language is he speaking? Sounds pretty! Ziz asks.

He is probably speaking in Sinhala or Tamil. On our flight, I read that those are the top two languages spoken here. English is common in urban areas and amongst interpreters and important officials, Fernando explains.

You are right! Pradeep agrees. He is speaking in Sinhala. Tamil is almost exclusively spoken in northern and eastern parts of the island, while Sinhala is widely spoken in the southern, western, and central parts of the country.

Gayan paces back and forth as he frantically speaks out loud.

He thinks that the replica was stolen while he was getting Gamini, his Maligawa elephant, ready for the first part of the celebration, says Pradeep. He will get in trouble for losing it. You see, the preparation involves putting special garments on the elephants. Gamini was supposed to carry the relic on a canopy on its back. Someone must have taken it while Gayan was dressing the elephant.

What is a Maligawa elephant? Ziz asks.

The name Maligawa is taken from the temple Kandy Sri Dalada Maligawa. These elephants belong to the temple, says the interpreter.

Why elephants? Wonders Ziz. Why not use any other animal?

In Buddhism, elephants and humans share strong connections. The elephant is a sign of strength, honor, patience, peacefulness, and wisdom. Let me show you a picture from the book I bought from the airport, says Fernando.

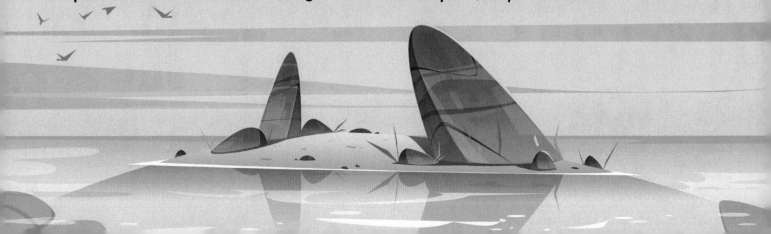

Where did Gayan last see the relic? Can I take a look at where it went missing? Fernando asks Gayan through the interpreter.

Of course! Follow me! Says Gayan.

Ziz follows everyone as they walk to the Temple of the Tooth Relic and sees monks in orange outfits.

We have spent so much time preparing for this parade, and now the tooth is gone, Gayan says to the other people. But help has arrived!

I will do whatever it takes to find the relic! Fernando says with confidence.

Please check out the temple and the alleys nearby, Fernando asks Ziz.

Ziz flies out, perches on top of a building, looks down an alley, and sees two men sneaking around and trying to hide something under what appears to be a sparkly red blanket. One of them is tall and thin with short hair, and the other is short with long curly hair.

That doesn't look right at all, Ziz says to himself.

Ziz flies back inside. In the alleyway, I saw two suspicious-looking men hiding something under a red blanket.

Fernando notices that one of the elephants is missing a garment. He examines the elephant and finds a strand of long curly hair on him.

Hmm... I see. Fernando says.

It does not make any sense! This elephant doesn't have a caretaker to dress him, says Pradeep.

Fernando points to the other elephants' garments and asks Ziz: The blanket you saw... Did it look like these?

Yes! These look exactly like the blanket I saw the two men carrying. A tall man and a short man. One with short hair, and the other with long curly hair. They are hiding something! Ziz says.

Pradeep interprets what is being said to Gayan.

Oh no! I know them, Says Gayan to Paradeep. There have been reports of jewels being stolen from vendors nearby, and those men fit the description.

Ziz, Please go back right away! They could be our thieves! Says Fernando with a loud voice. Pradeep, please call the police and tell them we may have the relic thieves.

Pradeep explains the situation to Gayan and calls the local police station.

Ziz flies back to the alley and watches the men from the top.

A car enters the alley.

Ziz sees something shiny flashing at him. He flies down closer and sees bits of jewels in the back of the car, barely visible through its rear window. The driver notices Ziz spying on him and quickly covers the jewels, and tries to drive away.

Ziz finds a nearby fruit stand and knocks over a big load of large watermelons, blocking the car's path.

The driver gets out and starts picking up the watermelons and putting them back on the fruit stand.

What are you doing?! You are not supposed to drive your car here! You need to pay for the watermelons! Says the fruit vendor, looking upset.

The driver refuses to pay.

By this time, a crowd of people gather around and block both sides of the road.

The car cannot move forward or backward.

Ziz flies back to the temple.

A car came by, but I stopped it! The two men in the alley that were holding the red sparkly blanket saw the car getting stuck. They looked worried! Says the excited Ziz.

Cars are not supposed to drive this way during the parade. They must be the thieves we are looking for! Gayan says.

And the blankets are woven cloaks, Pradeep explains. At the temple, people like Gayan work very hard to make these sequined outfits. And only a specially selected elephant can carry the canopy containing the replica of the relic.

Oh yes, the cloak was red with sparkly bits. The men I saw in the alley were hiding something under it! Ziz confirms.

Pradeep looks concerned. What will happen if we don't find the relic in time?

That will not be an option! We must find the relic, Gayan says.

They walk to the entrance of the temple.

Fernando takes out his magnifying glass and spots faint handprints on the wall near the entrance and bits of red fabric fibers on the ground. He takes a step forward and sees muddy footprints trailing from outside of the temple and into the streets.

Just what I thought, Fernando says to his friends. Ziz, please fly up and see if you can spot the suspicious people you saw earlier. Tell me if they have dirty hands and muddy shoes.

They all go to the alley near the temple.

Ziz flies up high into the sky and looks at the people below. He finds the men.

Ziz flies back down and lands on Pradeep's shoulder.

I saw them! They're a few stalls that way, Ziz says while pointing to the left. And Yes! I could see that one of them had muddy shoes!

Let's go, before they get away! Ziz says.

Fernando, Gayan and Pradeep follow Ziz.

They hide behind boxes in the alley and watch as the two men uncover what they were hiding. It is the relic!

One of them has dirty fingers and the other has muddy footprints!

Pradeep sighs. I've seen these two guys before. The tall one never wipes his hands clean after eating at the Kottu stall, and the other one always forgets to clean his shoes after stepping in elephants' poop! They have both been caught before for stealing jewels and other valuables from local shops.

I hope the policemen get here on time, says Pradeep as he takes a deep breath.

The policemen arrive.

But why would they steal the tooth relic? Ziz wonders.

Legend has it that the ones who hold the relic will be named royalty. But it doesn't work like that anymore. You cannot steal an ancient relic replica like this one, and expect to be royalty! Fernando says, laughing.

Pradeep calls over the policemen and a few of the temple members. They swiftly arrest the men in the alley. The driver tries to run but is caught by a policeman.

When the policemen unlock the car, they uncover dozens of stolen jewels and religious artifacts.

How did we get caught?! Our plan was foolproof! The tall thieve asks. His shirt has the same food stains as his hands.

You forgot to clean up after spilling delicious food on your shirt! Ziz laughs.

You have been stealing from different temples and vendors, haven't you?! That's not okay. Thank you everyone for helping us catch them. We won't let them get away this time, the head policeman says.

That solves the mystery of the missing tooth relic! Fernando says as Ziz rests on his shoulder.

Another mystery is in the bag! Says Ziz, looking proud.

Now, the festival can go on! Fernando says to Pradeep, Gayan, and the other temple members.

Fernando and Ziz celebrate their well-done job with a tasty plate of Kottu.

Pradeep invites them to watch the festival.

They watch as a special elephant carries the relic on his back while wearing a beautiful woven cloak that was recovered from the thieves earlier.

The elephant is very calm and gentle while walking through the crowd. Everyone looks up and admires him.

Fernando and Ziz decide to stay a few more days and do some sightseeing.

Pradeep, where should we visit before we leave? Asks Fernando.

There are plenty of things to do in Sri Lanka for everyone. If you don't have much time, I suggest seeing Sri Lanka's beautiful landscape from above in a hot air balloon. You need to go early in the morning. Here, I wrote down where to go and what to do in the next few days, says Pradeep as he hands Fernando a piece of paper.

Gayan and I want to see you before you leave if that is ok with you. We can meet you at the airport.

Absolutely! Ziz and Fernando say enthusiastically. See you at the airport!

Fernando and Ziz thank Pradeep and Gayan, catch a flight to the historic city of Galle, and stay at a hotel near the beach for the night.

The next day, as the sun comes up Ziz and Fernando float across mountains and jungles in a hot air balloon. An aerial view of Galle, with its ancient fort that still stands to this day, provides a unique experience.

Wow! What an unforgettable experience! A different kind of flying! I love it! Ziz says.

You are right! It was magical! I had never done this before, and will never forget it. This is a gorgeous country! Says the happy Fernando.

Afterward, they visit Galle Fort, walk around the city, and enjoy delicious Sri Lankan food.

Later in the afternoon, Fernando looks at the note that Pradeep gave them.
Hey Ziz, how about we do something different tomorrow!

What do you mean? Wonders Ziz.

Let's climb to the Top of Sigiriya!

Top of what?! Ziz asks looking confused.

Pradeep writes in his notes that Sigiriya is probably the country's most recognizable landmark, Sigiriya means "Lion's Rock" in Sinhalese. It is a **5th**-century fort and palace and a UNESCO World Heritage Site

That will be great! Says Ziz. But you have longer legs. What do I do if I get tired?!

Ziz, I think you forgot that you are a bird! You can always fly! Laughs Fernando.
Oh, you are right! Haha! I can always fly up! Ziz smiles. What are we waiting for?!
Let's go!

They hop on a train. Four and a half hours later they are in Sigiriya. After resting for the night they get up early the next morning.
There are **1,217** steps to the top. They walk between a pair of giant, carved lion's paws, take some pictures, pass by monks' ancient paintings on the rock, and reach the top.

Amazing! What a dazzling view of the valley below us! Says the tired Ziz.
Yes, it is! And I am proud of you. You walked all the way up! Fernando comments.
After resting for a while, they go back down.
It was a lot easier going down! Ziz tells Fernando.
For sure! Fernando says, feeling satisfied with their adventure for the day.

Ziz, we are leaving tomorrow. Do you like to follow Pradeep's suggestions, or do you like to do something different today? Asks Fernando.

Let me see his note please, Ziz asks politely. We have never done any surfing before. What do you think?

You are right! Pradeep wrote that Sri Lanka's southwest coast is great for beginner surfers. And the waves are not huge!

They pack their bags and catch a plane from Kandy. Ninety minutes later they land in Hikkaduwa.

After hiring a local instructor, Fernando and Ziz spend most of the day practicing riding the waves.
This is fantastic! I never knew surfing could be so much fun! Screams Ziz with joy.

Oh yeah! I am having the time of my life! Agrees Fernando.

By afternoon, they are both exhausted and very hungry.

Our flight tomorrow leaves late afternoon. We could spend the night here, Says Ziz. I couldn't agree more! Says Fernando.

They thank their instructor, eat delicious Sri Lankan food, and stay at a hotel for the night.

The following day Fernando and Ziz ride a taxi for their two-hour trip from Hikkaduwa to Bandaranaike International Airport.

Pradeep and Gayan meet our friends before their departure.

We could not solve the mystery of the missing relic without your help. Thank you! Ziz and Fernando say to their new friends.

We appreciate you coming to Sri Lanka! Have a safe trip! Says Gayan.

They shake hands, hug, and take a picture together.

On the picture is stamped: Another Mystery Solved...

Another Mystery Solved...

Fernando is a private detective,
Ziz, a parrot, is his partner and friend.
They investigate mysteries around the world,
And always solve them in the end.

The Kandy Esala Perahera parade
The Festival of the Tooth
Held each year in Sri Lanka
Is highlighted on the news.

As they are watching the coverage
The reporter has her microphone grabbed.
A man yells, I need the help of Fernando and Ziz,
The sacred tooth has been nabbed!

The Kandy Esala Perahera
Cannot happen this year
Without the Buddha's sacred tooth relic,
The parade must be canceled I fear.

Fernando and Ziz are famous,
They solve cases no one else could,
Like the golden jewelled shoe in Malaysia,
The police, alone, aren't as good.

So, Fernando and Ziz catch an airplane,
And direct to Sri Lanka they fly,
To help find this sacred tooth relic
That the country values so high.

They meet Gayan, the man who had called them,
Who takes them to the temple where the relic was lost.
It was stolen while the elephants were being dressed,
It must be found at all cost.

We'll find the relic, Fernando replied,
Ziz, will you please check the alleys nearby?
Ziz is happy to do as he is asked,
He is the only one who could fly.

Ziz perches on the roof of a building,
And sees two men acting sneaky and sly,
Hiding something in a shiny red blanket.
So back to his friend he flies.

They gather evidence, and detain the thieves
With the help of the crowd and the police.
They retrieve the tooth relic, other artifacts too.
Gayan and the monks are so pleased.

Another mysterious case has been solved,
So they decide to stay for awhile.
To sample Sri Lanka's wonderful food,
And check out the country in style.

They fly across jungles in a hot air balloon,
And they climb the famous Lion's Rock.
Passing between giant carved lion's paws,
It is over **12** hundred steps to the top.

Before going home they decide to surf,
So they go to Hikkaduwa on the coast.
They spend all day surfing and have so much fun,
Ziz seems to enjoy it the most.

The country is amazing, the food is as well.
It's such fun to explore the world.
Fernando never knows where he'd go next,
But travel is great, Boys and Girls.

65744107R00033